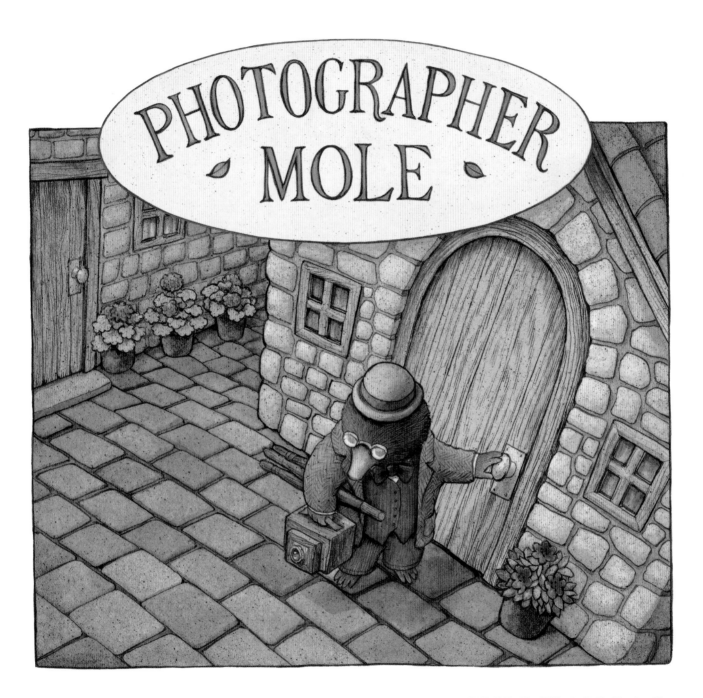

PHOTOGRAPHER
MOLE

DENNIS HASELEY ● illustrated by **JULI KANGAS**

Dial Books for Young Readers New York

Published by Dial Books for Young Readers
A division of Penguin Young Readers Group
345 Hudson Street
New York, New York 10014

Designed by Nancy R. Leo-Kelly
Text set in Hoefler Text
Manufactured in China on acid-free paper
1 3 5 7 9 10 8 6 4 2

Library of Congress Cataloging-in-Publication Data
Haseley, Dennis.
Photographer Mole / Dennis Haseley ; illustrated by Juli Kangas.
p.   cm.
Summary: The work of Mole the photographer is cherished by his neighbors,
but he decides that he must take a trip to discover the something
that is missing in his photographs.
ISBN 0-8037-2924-3
[1. Photographers—Fiction. 2. Happiness—Fiction.
3. Moles (Animals)—Fiction. 4. Animals—Fiction.}
I. Kangas, Juli, ill. II. Title.
PZ7.H2688PH 2004   [E]—dc21   2003003529

The artwork was prepared using ink, watercolor, and oil wash.

For Claudia and Connor —D. H.

For Georgia and Eric —J. K.

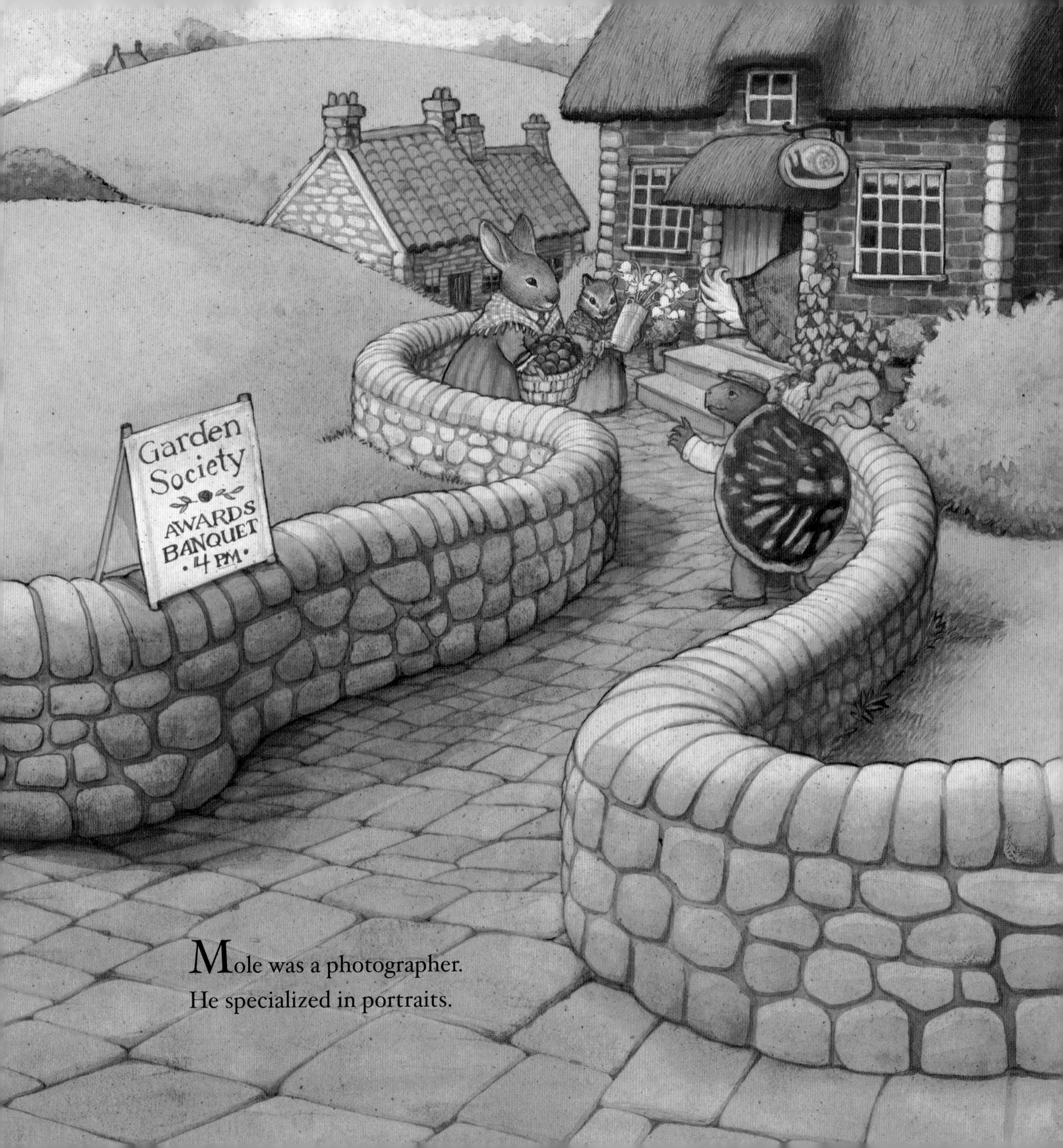
Garden Society
AWARDS BANQUET
·4 PM·

Mole was a photographer.
He specialized in portraits.

Whenever there was an important occasion for his neighbors, Mole was ready with his camera.

He was a popular guest at dinner, where he told
entertaining stories about the challenges of his work:
how the Rabbits needed quiet so as not to be jumpy,
and that the Pigs looked their best in the soft glow
of sunset.

But even though his fine photographs hung in every
home, Mole was not completely satisfied.

One evening, as he glanced from one of his portraits to the smiling family around the table, he realized that something was missing.

After he helped put the dinner dishes away, Mole walked home down the dark lane, alone.

When he got to his studio, he looked at his favorite portraits.
There was the Pig reunion. Commander Bear on his birthday.

The gathering of the Porcupine choir.

Something was missing in these pictures too. And Mole didn't know what it was.

The next afternoon, as he was snapping the Lawyer Swans, he threw back the camera's hood and stepped into the light of his studio.

"This needs to be fixed," he said.

"Should I move to the left?" asked the youngest Swan.

"No. Something is definitely absent," Mole said, feeling grave.

That evening, he paced around his room, looking
from picture to picture. And the more he looked, the
sadder he felt.

The next morning he hung a sign on his shop that said:

CLOSED FOR REPAIRS.

He packed his suitcase.

As word got out, his neighbors tried to convince him to stay.

"This is a wonderful likeness of me," said Commander Bear.
"You can even see the starch in my collar."

"Yes," said Mole faintly. "But it could be brighter."

"You've posed us so calmly in this one," said the Rabbits,
"that our thoughtfulness shows."

"And you've perfectly captured our delicate snouts," said the Pigs.

But as the animals glanced from Mole to the pictures he had taken, they began to understand that what he was troubled by was more than a matter of starch or snouts or poses.

They gathered to say good-bye to Mole at the train station, asking when he would be back.

"When I find what's missing in my pictures," said Mole. His small eyes seemed far away.

As the cars pulled out, the Rabbits and Pigs, the Porcupines and Bears tried to make sense of his leaving.

"Perhaps if he tries another camera."

"Or perhaps if he takes pictures of other sights."

"Other sights?" said the Pigs. "Besides us?"

"Besides me?" harrumphed Commander Bear.

Weeks wore on.
There was an empty place
at the dinner tables. The Rabbits told
how Mole always managed to keep them still,
and the Pigs talked about how he always waited for evening
to pose them. But it wasn't the same without Mole telling it.

The animals all hoped Mole was finding whatever he was looking for, but the photographs and notes he sent didn't show that anything had changed.

Meanwhile, the Sheep jubilee was never captured on film.

No one was there to photograph the Bulldog reunion.

And, as more time went by, his neighbors worried that when Mole finally found what he was looking for, he might not return to them.

Then, one day, another photograph arrived: It was a cheery picture of a flower.

The note that came with it gave only the date and time of Mole's arrival.

On that day, the entire town came to the station.

They waited expectantly as the train chugged to a stop.

And the door to the passenger car opened.

After a long moment, Mole walked down the steps.

He had the same old camera in his hand, and he was
wearing a new suit.

"Welcome home!" they shouted. "Did you find it? Did you
find what was missing?"

"Yes, I did," he said.

At the bottom of the steps, he turned.

In the door of the train was the flower from the photo, its
long stem traveling down to a hat.

And under the hat, stepping into the doorway as if she were
entering a frame, was a mole in a long yellow dress.

"This is Belinda," Mole said. "My bride-to-be. She has
shown me what I've been leaving out."

The wedding was held in the town hall.

You can still see the reception in this picture hanging on
the wall at the Moles' house, next to the photo of the wedding
couple that Mole arranged to take himself. (It was something
he'd learned on his travels.)

And as you can also see, this was the first of many times
that Mole himself looked out from a photograph—

smiling.